Solomon Scarecrow
and the Great Rescue

For Luke, Reuben, Jude, Caleb and Jaiden.
My whole world. I love you more
than you will ever know x x x

Matador
9 Priory Business Park,
Wistow Road, Kibworth Beauchamp,
Leicestershire. LE8 0RX
Tel: 0116 279 2299
Email: books@troubador.co.uk
Web: www.troubador.co.uk/matador
Twitter: @matadorbooks

ISBN 978 1800460 867

British Library Cataloguing in Publication Data.
A catalogue record for this book is available from the British Library.

Printed and bound by CPI Group (UK) Ltd, Croydon, CR0 4YY
Typeset in 18pt Stez Sans by Troubador Publishing Ltd, Leicester, UK

Matador is an imprint of Troubador Publishing Ltd

Solomon Scarecrow
and the Great Rescue

A scarecrow wandered through his field one day,
Hoping to find a friend.
He ran through the tall grass, beside a small stream,
And over the hilly bend.

He came to a duck pond, all splashy and wet,
With three little ducks in a row.
"Excuse me," he shouted, "will you be my friend?
My name is Solomon Scarecrow."

The ducks looked at the scarecrow, full of stuffing and straw,
Then looked at each other and sighed.
"You're too messy and scruffy and straggly for us,
Please leave us alone," they cried.

The scarecrow wandered through his field one day,
Still hoping to find a friend.
He walked through the tall grass, beside a small stream,
And over the hilly bend.

He came to some marsh land, all squelchy and green,
With one little frog, small and slow.
"Excuse me," he chanted, "will you be my friend?
My name is Solomon Scarecrow."

The frog looked at the scarecrow, all tatty and torn,
Then shook his head very fast.
"You're too dusty and lazy and boring for me,
Now please, just walk on past."

The scarecrow wandered
through his field one day,
Still wanting to find a friend.

He shuffled through
the tall grass,

Beside a small stream,

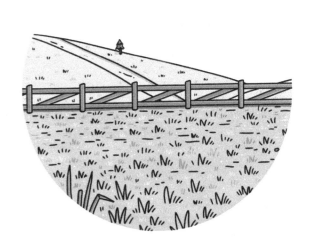

And over the hilly bend.

He came to a hen house, all clucky and loud,

With feathery hens on the go.

"Excuse me," he muttered, "will you be my friend?

My name is Solomon Scarecrow."

The hens looked at the scarecrow, all mucky and drab,

Then looked at the ground with a cough.

"You're too lonely and fearful and silent for me,

Now please, go away, clear off."

The scarecrow wandered through his field one day,
Not hoping to find a friend.
He crept through the tall grass, beside a small stream,
And over the hilly bend.

A small rabbit appeared, looking startled and scared,
Darting from side to side.
"Excuse me," he yelled out, "a fox wants to eat me,
Do you know where I can hide?"

The scarecrow thought quickly and opened his coat.

"In here, hide in my straw."

The rabbit hopped in and made himself hidden,

Then the scarecrow hid him some more.

The pair hurried back,
the fox hot on their tail,
Running past the hen house
once more.
"Fox! Fox!" shrieked the
rabbit, alarming the hens,
Causing panic and
mayhem galore.

Quick as a flash, the scarecrow rolled up his sleeves,
And pulled the straw hat from his head.
"Quick, hens, hide in here," the brave scarecrow invited,
And they all piled in as they fled.

The group hurried on, the fox trailing behind,
And they came to the home in the swamp.
"Fox! Fox!" the hens screamed to the frog as he slept,
And he woke with a ribbit and stomp.

The quick-thinking scarecrow tore off one boot,
And gestured toward the inside.
"Quick, frog, hide in here," the kind scarecrow invited,
And the frog dived in for the ride.

On stumbled the scarecrow, now starting to tire,
When the duck pond came into view.
"Fox! Fox!" the frog croaked to the ducks as they splashed,
And they made such a hullabaloo!

The now-frantic scarecrow opened his coat once again,
And found a gap at the side.
"Quick, ducks, hide in here," the helpful scarecrow invited,
And they jumped in quacking, wide-eyed.

The scarecrow moved slowly with his cargo on board,
Weighing him down as he went.
The fox tried to follow, but found it a struggle,
As he could no longer follow the scent.

The scarecrow, though weary, looked at the animals he'd saved,
Clambering back round the bend.
"My name is Solomon Scarecrow," he whispered,
"Will anyone here be my friend?"

"I will," hollered the frog
from inside the boot,
"You're brave and
kind and true."

"Us too," quacked the ducks,
beaks poking out of the straw,
"You're selfless through
and through."

The hens clucked excitedly
from somewhere inside,
"We'd be honoured to call
you our friend."

"You saved me," said the
rabbit, big ears peeking out,
"Our friendship will
never end!"

The scarecrow smiled as he arrived back home,
And took up his spot on the land,

The animals climbed out, one at a time,
And shook our Solomon's hand.

The night drew in, and the friends headed home,
The scarecrow let out a big sigh.

"My name is Solomon Scarecrow," he beamed,

"And I'll never be lonely, not I!"